T0123401

Puttins, Path and Peril

DARRYL DESHUN BULLOCK

WESTBOW
PRESS®
A DIVISION OF THOMAS NELSON
& ZONDERVAN

WestBow Press books may be ordered through booksellers or by contacting:

WestBow Press
A Division of Thomas Nelson & Zondervan
1663 Liberty Drive
Bloomington, IN 47403
www.westbowpress.com
1 (866) 928-1240

This is a work of fiction. All of the characters, names, incidents,
organizations, and dialogue in this novel are either the products
of the author's imagination or are used fictitiously.

ISBN: 978-1-9736-5573-2 (sc)
ISBN: 978-1-9736-5574-9 (e)

Library of Congress Control Number: 2019902491

Print information available on the last page.

WestBow Press rev. date: 03/26/2019

Dedication

I dedicate this book to my loving wife, TeriLynn. I want to thank my daughter, Deia, for all the wonderful ideas she gave to me. I thank my daughter, Natalia, for her help typing the manuscript. I thank Diane, Arlene and Leonard for their invaluable feedback. And, I want to thank my mom for her understanding. And last but not least, I am grateful to you, the reader.

I am excited and honored that Kidd Coyote illustrated the book. She is a great artist, and I hope you enjoy her art as much as I do. Thank you KC!

Anna asleep on the path

Chapter 1

Once upon a time, there was a 10-year-old girl named Anna. She was tall for her age and her hair was dark brown and naturally curled into ringlets. She always kept her hair in braids to keep from having to brush it. She had beautiful, sensitive, shy brown eyes, olive colored skin, and a mischievous smile. She lived with her mother and father in a beautiful town in Washington. On the night this story begins, Anna and her father were upstairs playing a game of chess. After the game was over Anna's father said, "Time to go to bed, dear."

"Yes, Daddy," Anna answered, and hurried off to bed.

She smiled as her daddy called, 'I love you," down the hall after her.

"I love you, too, Daddy!" Anna responded.

Anna went to her bedroom and began daydreaming. "Oh, I hope for an adventure someday soon," she wished out loud, hugging herself in anticipation. She was tired of the same old stuff day after day, get up, go to school, Anna wanted something exciting to happen.

Anna's mother came into her room to tuck her into

bed. They knelt down together beside the bed and took turns praying. With all her heart Anna prayed:

Dear Lord, oh heavens light,
Please come visit me tonight.

Give me adventure to my heart's content.
Oh please, let me camp and sleep in a tent.

You are my alpha and omega,
You are my all and all.

So please in your greatness,
Do not stall.
Amen!

Anna saw her mother smile at her prayer, but did not understand the wisdom behind the smile. She felt her mother's kiss on her forehead as she was tucked into bed. "I love you, Anna," her mother told her, with a chuckle in her voice.

***

Far away from Anna, in a magical land, there lived a great king. The king lived in a golden palace in the City of the Clouds and served the one true God. He was called the "Great King" because he was the oldest angel who was Lord over all who lived in the City of the Clouds, and over all of the lands of that magical world. Nothing escaped his attention.

The city was located in the sky, in magical clouds. Angels lived there with fairies, and cloud people. Below the clouds, many strange and wonderful people and animals lived in the Land of Dreams. Perhaps some of the most interesting were the Little People and the Puttins.

The Little People lived in a village located in a thick rain forest, teaming with all sorts of animal and plant life. They were graceful, slender people about 3 feet tall. They lived a very simple tribal life, wearing animal skins, cooking over fires, and building simple huts. When they spoke, a funny thing happened with their voice. It sounded like they made a soft "T" sound before the first word of each sentence. At the time this story takes place, they were enemies to the Puttins.

The Puttins were small in height, also. But, they were not slender; they were jolly and round. They liked to jump and roll through the air like a ball, especially when they were fighting their enemies, the Little People. They also lived a very simple tribal life, similar to the Little People. When they spoke, their voice made a soft "P" sound before the first word of their sentences.

The fighting that took place between the Puttins and the Little People was a cause of concern to the Great King. For this reason, he called forth his advisory council to a meeting; he invited the Angel Generals and the Fairy Royalty to discuss how to make peace between the two warring tribes. The meeting of the advisory council took place in the golden palace in the City of the Clouds above the Land of Dreams.

The Great King and both his leading generals, the Angel General Xar and the Angel General Carl, were present to discuss the issue between the Little People and the Puttins in a room made of pure gold. The Royal Fairy, Prince Stan walked into the room and the meeting began.

Angel General Xar suggested to the Great King, "We should rule the Land of Dreams by force, then we can bring order and make everything right."

Prince Stan presented his view, "You cannot rule by force; all living beings should have the freedom to make their own mistakes and learn from them. If living beings are not free to choose their own path and then learn life's lessons, at the end they will not be happy."

The Great King pondered as the debate continued. Then he said, "Everybody leave except Prince Stan."

Angel Carl, his loyal general, left obediently. Angel General Xar, who was annoyed by the meeting, slowly left. When they were both gone, the Great King told Prince Stan, "God spoke to my heart and told me to bring Anna to the Land of Dreams."

"Who is Anna," asked the fairy Prince.

"Anna is a human from another world. God showed me the prayer of her heart. She asked for an adventure, and I'm going to give it to her. Her heart is kind, and I believe that she has the compassion the Puttins and The Little

People need as both of my tribes hit a dangerous time in their history."

"They need guidance to make the right decisions," Prince Stan agreed. "We fairies stand ready to assist you my King, and my friend." The Fairy bowed to the King with respect.

As Stan left his chamber, the King gathered all of his magic to transport Anna to the Land of Dreams. He closed his eyes and was in deep meditation with God as the room was darkened.

***

As Anna fell asleep she drifted off to a distant land: a land of dreams and adventure; a land of excitement!

"Come, come, come…" a voice seemed to say.

It was in her, and around her. Then something *flashed* a blinding, white light!

Anna awoke suddenly out of the dream. She was lying on the ground on a beautiful forest path! The Great King in his golden palace smiled at the results of his magic.

Magical rainbow fly cave

Chapter 2

Anna jumped up and looked around. Clapping in glee, she said out loud, "God answered my prayer! No school today!" Then she started exploring the path a little.

Sights, sounds, and scents of the old rain forest surrounded Anna. The magic path that she awoke upon was winding its way through huge trees. Anna couldn't see very far down the path because the forest was thick with vegetation.

Feeling a little scared because she was alone, Anna began to walk down the path. When she observed little chipmunks playing in a tree, she laughed to herself. One chipmunk took food from another, it was so cute. Then she saw a little baby chipmunk nibbling on an acorn. "That's just the cutest little thing!" Anna thought to herself.

A pretty little bird perched in the branch above her. Anna slowly walked toward the bird and stopped right in front of him. The bird, curious about Anna, cocked his head sideways. Anna whistled, and the bird chirped in return, and then flew off. Anna sprinted after him. She laughed as she chased him. But soon, the bird flew out of site.

About this time, Anna was starting to get a little worried, "Where will I get food and water?" she asked herself. Anna pushed her worry aside and decided to trust in God because she knew He brought her to this place and so would keep her safe and provide for her. She made up her mind that no matter what, she would be joyful. Anna hoped someone would find her and help her.

Pretty soon, Anna noticed one little pink fly following her as she walked. It wasn't just a normal housefly. It was beautiful. Then, a blue one joined her and did a little "fly dance." One at a time, more little rainbow flies flew with her as she walked. They were all the colors of the rainbow. They buzzed, chirped, and danced happily as Anna walked.

Laughing at their antics, Anna asked the flies, "Will I ever get home?" They chirped back at her.

Just then, one of the flies, a pink one, flew in and perched herself on Anna's shoulder. The fly held a little droplet of magic honey. Anna carefully took the honey on her finger and tasted it. The honey filled her with joy.

Anna followed the flies through a berry patch. The patch was just off the path. Anna grabbed some berries to eat and they were yummy to her tummy. The flies led her through the berry patch to their rainbow cave. Outside of the cave, the flies surrounded her and chirped in unison a little fly song. The girl flies chirped the melody while the boy flies chirped the harmony; it was a pretty song that made Anna's heart dance.

A beam of sunlight glimmered through the tropical greenery. The ray hit the entrance of the cave creating a beautiful moment. Anna stepped into the cave and saw a clear pool. She thought it was water but was quite surprised to find out that it was actually honey. "Wow," she thought to herself. The pool sparkled like crystal and was clear to the eye. She sat down on a rock next to the pool to rest her legs. "This is beautiful," she exclaimed to the same pink fly who was still riding on her shoulder; she chirped back.

Anna rested for an hour enjoying the beauty of the magical rainbow fly cave. Then she ventured through the berry patch to get back to the path. It was magical, this beautiful, lush path that ran through the deep forest.

The pink fly was still on her shoulder making cute little noises. Anna felt a bond of friendship form with the sweet little fly. Now she knew she would no longer be alone. She felt a hum of hope as a light beam found its way through the thick branches, beaming cheerfully on her head. "Now I am ready for anything," she thought.

Then, she heard a rustle in the trees. Anna was startled at first, and she tried in vain to peer through the thick forest to see what had made the noise. The pink fly purred and the vibration filled Anna's heart with courage.

Crash

A little man jumped out of the trees pointing a stick at her, which appeared to be a spear. He was hairy and unkempt, and his clothes were made from animal skins. He looked completely savage.

Anna jumped back a little.

"T-are you a Puttin?" the little man demanded.

Anna was amazed that she could understand him. "No, I'm not. What is a Puttin?"

"T-come with me," the little man demanded, raising his spear and ignoring Anna's question. "T-come with me," he repeated, "T-you're my prisoner!"

"Prisoner! What did I do?" Anna asked, appalled. Again ignoring Anna, the little man escorted her along the forest path at spear point.

They gazed down onto a village

Chapter 3

After an hour of walking with Anna at spear point, the little man veered off the path through some thick trees; they could not see ahead. Anna stroked the little rainbow fly on her shoulder for comfort.

Suddenly, they came to a hut made of branches and leaves. It was about as big as a tent. "T-stop," the little man commanded. Startled, she stopped. But she was very curious and wondered if someone lived in the hut.

The door to the hut flew open and another little man came out. "T-who is this," he demanded.

"T-I found this girl wandering in the forest, and she is my T-prisoner," the little warrior stated proudly.

The little person in front of the door frowned. "T-we need to be more hospitable to the human!" he told the warrior.

"Thank goodness," thought Anna.

Then the little man turned to Anna and said, "T-my name is Tear." Tear motioned for the other little man to lower his spear and said, "T-his name is Towel. T-we are

The Little People. T-we are on the watch for strangers who could be helping the Puttins attack us."

"What is a Puttin?" asked Anna.

"T-Puttins are our T-enemies," replied Tear.

"T-we are at war with them," Towel blurted out angrily.

"T-we need to take you to our village," Tear said. He led the way and Anna followed, still wondering what a Puttin was. Towel followed with spear in hand.

The three continued along the forest path. The path went up a hill and then started down the other side. Ten minutes later the woods opened up into a clearing and they gazed down onto a village. Anna saw a bunch of little straw huts about the size of tents. There were many Little People out in an open area that looked like a town square.

Anna's little friend, the sweet little pink fly, squeaked encouragingly on her shoulder as they walked toward the center of the village.

"Wow, what an adventure!" Anna thought as she gratefully stroked her newly adopted friend.

"T-let's go," Tear motioned both Anna and Towel to step forward. The whole town surrounded them; over a hundred Little People.

Anna listened as Tear turned to address the villagers, "T-this is a human girl we found on the path, wandering through the forest."

"T-she is here to destroy us!" someone yelled out.

"T-she is siding with our T-enemies," another chimed in.

"T-she is a Puttin," the crowed bellowed.

Anna started to feel afraid, but then Tear motioned the crowd to calm down. "T-she is not a Puttin, T-she is human," he said.

Towel gave Anna suspicious looks, not trusting her; and Anna lowered her eyes, shyly.

As the crowd gathered around, they observed Anna's innocent, girlish demeanor. A lady stepped forward from the crowd. She smiled and said, "T-my name is Tan, T-what's your name?"

"Anna," she responded with an answering smile.

Another female stepped forward and exchanged smiles with Anna, "T-I am Tut."

"T-see, everybody? T-she is not our enemy," Tear declared, looking pointedly at Towel, who shuffled his toe in the dirt and pretended not to see.

A cute little couple caught Anna's eye, and introduced themselves, "T-hi, T-I am Tom and this is my wife Tia."

"It's nice to meet you," said Anna sweetly.

Then Anna felt a tug on her hand, "T-come to my hut," Tan said, and she led Anna away from the crowd; the little pink fly chirped in excitement. Tan's home was on the far side of the village.

Tan had light skin with blond hair; she was wearing leggings and a shirt made from animal skins. She looked rustic, but was graceful and had pretty, blue eyes. "T-where are you from?"

"A little town in a place called Washington," Anna replied.

"T-would you like something to eat?" Tan asked her.

"Yes, I'm so hungry I could eat a whole ham myself!" exclaimed Anna.

"T-what is a ham?" Tan asked. But Anna didn't answer because she was entering Tan's hut. Tan's hut was cozy and made of straw and animal skins. There was a chair that her father had lovingly made for her, and a tiny table. There was also a bed that was big enough for two.

"T-we have some meat and plants for you. T-and here is some fresh water for you."

Anna suddenly realized how thirsty she was and drained the container of water. Then she greedily ate the food offered to her until she was full. The meat was a little tough and the plants were sour, but she was too hungry to care.

After the meal, Anna yawned and stretched sleepily. "T-time to go to bed. We can talk more tomorrow," Tan told her.

Anna felt Tan tucking her in and she fell fast asleep.

"T-let's drink."

Chapter 4

When Anna woke up in the morning, she heard Tan preparing breakfast. "Something smells yummy," said Anna, sniffing the air. Her pink friend agreed.

"T-did you sleep well?" Tan asked.

"Very well, thank you," Anna politely responded.

They ate eggs and vegetables for breakfast and drank water. The pink fly sipped nectar from the flowers outside. Then Anna got up, washed her face, and helped Tan make up the bed.

"T-I never had very many visitors over," Tan told Anna, smiling. Anna returned Tan's smile. Tan said, "T-our leader, Tear, wants to talk to you in his hut right away."

"That will be great," Anna responded.

Tan and Anna walked through the village; it was a short walk to Tear's hut. Most of the Little People greeted her and her friends warmly as they passed by. But not Towel, and he followed them at a distance. "I guess he still doesn't trust me," thought Anna.

Just as they arrived at Tear's hut, Tom sprinted up to

them. "T-could you come to my hut, tonight? T-me and my mate would like to have you over for dinner."

Tan and Anna looked at each other. "T-do you want to?" Tan asked Anna. Anna felt shy and didn't know what to say. But she looked over at Tan and hoped Tan would answer for her.

"T-sure," Tan informed Tom. Anna felt happy about the plan and grinned at Tom and Tan.

"T-goodbye, T-see you tonight," Tom exclaimed and then sprinted away. Tan turned and knocked on Tear's door.

"T-come in! T-welcome to my hut," Tear happily greeted them. Anna was looking forward to getting to know Tear. "T-come over here," Tear called invitingly for Anna and Tan to join him.

Anna felt nervous as she and Tan approached Tear.

"T-did you have a good night's rest?" Tear asked Anna. "Yes I did. Tan was very nice to me," Anna said. "And breakfast was yummy," she added.

"T-we were well received by the towns people," Tan informed Tear. "T-and they enjoyed the little friend on Anna's shoulder."

"T-I'm glad to hear that everyone is getting along," Tear responded. "T-Time for tea, Ladies," Tear gestured towards the table.

Anna saw that the tea serving was already laid out on a small wooden table. Instead of a teapot, there was a wooden jug containing warm tea. At each chair, Tear had provided a small cup. Tear had even prepared a little place for the pink rainbow fly. There was a little leaf with a droplet of nectar carefully placed next to Anna's cup. The little pink fly settled on the leaf and sipped happily, making cute little noises of contentment.

Tear sat down and began to pour the tea; the ladies joined him at the table.

When he finished he said, "T-let's drink."

As Anna nervously took a dainty sip from her cup, she looked up just in time to see both Tear and Tan spit out the tea in unison. Anna gasped and her mouth fell open in shock. She jumped up out her chair and cried, "What are you doing?"

Tear and Tan looked at Anna, annoyed. "T-so, you don't like my tea!" Tear demanded.

All of Anna's nervousness fled, "I like your tea just fine," she declared.

Tan stood up, faced Anna, and squared her shoulders, "T-in our village, when you like someone's tea, you show it by spitting it out," she declared.

Anna was taken aback, "Oh, I'm sorry!" she said in an embarrassed voice.

"T-sit down ladies, T-please," Tear said. Anna saw that her apology made Tear happy.

Tan and Anna took their seats. Anna's fly friend, finished with her nectar, settled back on Anna's shoulder. Everyone picked up their cups again to continue the tea party.

Anna saw that Tear and Tan were watching her to see what she would do. So, she took a sip, filled her mouth with tea, and then spat it out on the floor of the hut.

Tear and Tan smiled at her and relaxed. The tea party was a success.

They ran through the planted fields

Chapter 5

After the early morning tea, Anna started walking with Tan back to Tan's home on the other side of the village.

Anna saw Towel across the town square and waved at him. Towel gave them a wicked scowl in response.

"T-what's his problem!" Tan commented out loud.

"I don't know," Anna frowned, she felt worried.

"T-we are almost home," Tan said. Anna smiled at Tan. Then the little pink fly chirped at her. Anna stroked the fly in response, and felt her mood lighten.

They finally reached Tan's hut. Tan was asking Anna questions about her adventures, Anna was answering, and the little pink fly was exploring Tan's hair when someone knocked on the door.

A voice called out, "T-hi, Honey! T-you know it's me, Turkey, the man of your dreams."

The little pink fly buzzed quickly to Anna as Tan jumped up and went to the door. "T-you know what happened the last time you tried to get friendly! T-I'll knock you out again!" she warned. Tan's eyes sparked like fire. Turkey left.

Anna couldn't help laughing and winking to her little fly friend.

Tan turned to her and said, "T-I want him gone!"

"For sure!" Anna agreed.

"Bzzzzz!" agreed Anna's companion.

They continued talking in Tan's hut for a while, getting to know each other.

"T-I want to show you where they grow plants for eating and making tea," Tan informed Anna.

"Oh, that sounds great," Anna replied with enthusiasm because she liked the idea of getting outside and moving about seeing how the village lived. They quickly left to visit the planting fields which were a mile outside of the village.

The first field they came to had green veggies, some bushy and wispy and some stalky and round. "T-these are our celery and carrots; we love planting," Tan explained as she showed Anna the fields.

"My mom likes to plant things, too," Anna responded.

Just then, a bunch of the kids from the village ran through the planted fields. "T-you little rascals! T-I'll get you!" Tan yelled.

"Let's join them!" Anna called. She took off and ran after them, the fly zooming after her.

"T-wait up!" Tan bellowed, and she bolted after Anna.

They joined the kids, laughing and playing until evening. They were tired when it was time to go to Tom and Tia's hut for dinner.

Tan knocked on Tom and Tia's door.

"T-please come in," Tia invited.

Tan and Anna came inside with the fly chirping happily. "T-oh, your fly friend is so cute," Tia exclaimed.

"I think so, too," Anna answered timidly.

Their hut had a lot more room than Tan's living space. It had a full wooden table with four wooden chairs. A restful king size bed was snug in the corner.

They all sat down to drink herbal tea. Anna, not wanting to disappoint again, spat the tea on the floor at the same time as Tan, Tia, and Tom spat out their tea. Tom smiled and said to both Tan and Anna, "T-I am so glad you like it."

They all ate carrots and meat until they were full. Tia, Tan, and Anna visited until bedtime.

"T-time to go to bed," Tan said as they left the hut.

When they got home, Anna made herself comfortable and Tan laid a blanket over her. Anna crooned a prayer.

Goodnight,
Dear God,
I pray for rest,
Until morning.

Then more thrills,
More excitement,
More fun,
Until the adventure ends.

Anna fell fast asleep next to her little fly friend who was such a comfort to her.

After the battle

Chapter 6

Bang
Smash
Bang

Anna woke up to a battle cry, "T-the Puttins are here!" Tan ran into her hut screaming, "T-get up; T-get up!"

Anna ran outside the straw hut, the pink fly on her shoulder. She saw the rest of the Little People running to the far edge of the village where the little warriors stood in battle array. Tear and Towel stood with about 30 warriors.

"T-get ready, T-here they come!" warned Tear.

The men were ready with spears in hand. Tan grabbed Anna's hand and pulled her to hide in the thickets, just off the path. "T-he is coming," Tan whispered.

A short, fat man sprinted up with a sword in hand. "P-charge!" he screamed.

Just then Anna observed 10 objects that looked like huge bowling balls. She saw one roll into Tom. He sprang up and threw his spear at the object, but he missed.

Anna and Tan trembled as they watched from their

hiding place. The fly clung faithfully to Anna's shoulder giving her strength.

"T-hold the line," Tear ordered as one of the balls rolled to a stop and stood up. It was another short, fat man. No taller than the Little People, but much, much fatter; he was so fat that he appeared to be a perfect bowling ball. He was a Puttin.

"P-meet me in combat!" the Puttin yelled.

Towel bellowed, "T-I'll meet you in combat!" He threw his spear at the short, fat man, missing him. But the Puttin dropped his miniature sword as Towel jumped on him and wrestled him to the ground.

"P-attack!" yelled the pinned Puttin.

Anna was terrified as she saw Tear turn around just in time to see 20 Puttins advancing and a ball heading straight for his head. Before Tear could duck, it smacked him on the head and he bellowed as he fell to the forest floor. "T-behind us!" he shouted.

Anna hid her head on Tan's shoulder to hide from the confusion of the battle. There were ball men bouncing in from all directions, slamming into huts, through the walls, and destroying as they came. The balls rolled to the center of town and stood up. They were all Puttins; the same short, fat, little men.

"P-do you surrender?" asked the Puttin who had led the charge, even though Towel still pinned him down.

"T-I'll never surrender!" Towel said defiantly.

Just then, 15 other big bowling balls smashed into Tear's warriors. "Retreat!" Tear yelled.

Another Puttin grabbed Towel in a choke hold and held a little sword with its tip poking into Towel's back. "P-you had better let him go," he warned. Towel raised his hands and he surrendered with a defiant glare.

Most of the Little People fled. The short fat man who had wrestled Towel was the leader. "P-round them up," he ordered, dusting the dirt off of himself.

The town of the Little People was in bad shape; all of the huts were smashed. Anna peeked out from the bushes at the damage as she stroked the little fly for comfort.

Tan whispered, "T-be quiet."

Tan and Anna held each other's hand for support. The little pink fly cuddled on Anna's shoulder.

Anna was trying to be quiet and move back a little, but her foot snapped a twig.

"P-What is that?" the one who led the charge asked. "P-go see what that is!"

Two of his men approached the bushes with swords drawn, "P-come out with your hands up."

Anna and Tan stepped out of the bushes with their hands raised up. One of the men barked, "P-who are you?" He pointed at Anna.

"I'm Anna," she responded in fright.

"P-you are my prisoner. P-come with me!" the soldier demanded.

With sword drawn, he escorted both of them to the

other Little People. Then, they made Tear, Towel, Tom, and the rest of them march away from the Little People's village.

Anna asked, "Who are you?"

The one who led the attack said, "P-we are the Puttins and I am Pat, leader of the Puttins. P-you are my prisoner."

"T-you cheated!" Towel bellowed glaring at Pat.

"P-shut your mouth," Pat ordered him.

The group of 30 Puttins escorted a group of 30 Little People with swords drawn. Pat said to Tear, "P-keep moving!"

"T-this isn't over," Tear bellowed.

"P-we'll lock you up in our prison," one of Pats men threatened.

Anna said, "Why are you doing this? You hurt a lot of people."

Pat replied, "P-we want access to the rainbow flies' cave, and the Little People won't give it to us."

Tear said, "T-we'll never give you access to the rainbow cave, leave the flies alone!"

"Stop it!" Anna blurted out. The little pink fly hid in Anna's shirt, trembling. Anna stroked her little friend to reassure her.

"P-I'll feed you to the wolves!" Pat threatened.

"That's not nice!" Anna rebuked the Puttin.

Pat turned away mumbling, "P-well, he's not nice to me!" Anna heard him say under his breath. Then he shouted, "P-move out!"

They walked for miles

Chapter 7

It was a sunny morning as they walked along the path to the Puttin village. The forest was filled with the sound of birds chirping and singing.

They walked for miles, and the sunny morning developed into a hot afternoon. The Puttins allowed short rest stops and shared water with their prisoners.

Late afternoon, they came to a small, circular meadow with bushes bordering all sides of it. Anna asked, "Where are we going?"

"P-be quiet!" Pat snapped.

While Anna distracted Pat, Tan whispered to Towel, "T-look!" She pointed to an opening in the bushes on the far side of the meadow that might give them an escape route.

Towel flew into action. He turned around and grabbed one of the Puttin warriors and began to wrestle him for his sword. Meanwhile, Tan grabbed Anna's arm and ran with her across the meadow through the opening in the bushes.

"Where are we going?" Anna panted. The little fly

chirped and flew around Anna's head in confusion because she didn't know what was happening.

"T-just go!" Tan replied as they went through the opening.

They heard shouts of pursuit behind them, "P-get them," "P-stop them!"

"No!" Pat ordered, "P-get back and guard the others, and set up camp. P-we'll pursue the runaways." Pat and one of his warriors followed Tan and Anna into the bushes.

The Puttin warriors did as they were told and stood guard over the rest of the Little People while setting up camp. Two warriors pinned down Towel, and one of them pointed a sword at his head.

"P-tie him up," another warrior ordered.

Anna and Tan weaved and ducked low through the thick under-bushes. Then, all of a sudden, Anna's right foot stepped into empty air. A huge hole! But, as quick as a thought, Tan grabbed her hand and pulled her to safety. They heard Pat and the other Puttin come near. "T-let's hide in those bushes," Tan whispered.

Pat and the warrior were advancing fast to catch Anna and Tan. "P-I'm going to make you pay for running!" Pat shouted. By the time they reached the hole that Anna avoided, they were moving too fast to save themselves. The warrior fell in first, and Pat landed on top of him. The hole was 10 feet deep!

Anna and Tan saw them fall. "T-let's leave them," urged Tan.

"No, we've got to help them," Anna stated firmly.

"T-we can get away," Tan argued.

"But they could be badly hurt," Anna told Tan.

Tan was frustrated, "T-why save them? T-all Pat is going to do is feed us to the wolves. T-we need to run! T-let Pat rot with the rest of the Puttins!"

Anna responded, "If we run, we are no better than the Puttins. We need to help Pat and the other soldier."

Tan threw her hands in the air, "T-I give up! T-what do you want me to do?"

"We should go down together to rescue them," Anna decided.

They found a rope in the bushes next to the hole that someone had obviously dug as an animal trap. Tan took one end of the rope and anchored it to a tree. Tan was a little woman, but was quite strong! As a matter of fact, she was one of the tougher females in her village. She was able to lower Anna down into the hole where the two Puttin warriors lay. The fly chirped with concern and worry, and flew around Anna's head as she descended. The air was thick with dust and it was hard to breathe.

When she reached the bottom, Anna grabbed Pat who was on the top of the Puttin pile. She tied the rope around him and checked to see if it was secure. Then Tan gave a little tug to see if the rope would hold, and she began hoisting him up.

Just as Pat's body lifted off the ground, he woke up

because of the pain and started to panic. The first person he saw was Anna. He immediately got a choke hold on her!

"P-you're trying to kill me!" Pat yelled.

The fly chirped loudly in agitation as she dive-bombed on Pat's hand around Anna's neck, and then bounced off harmlessly.

"No!" Anna gasped. Tan quickly jerked the rope, hard. Pat yelped and let go of Anna, and Anna jumped back out of the way.

"P-ouch, P-ouch!" Pat yelled.

Anna's face turned once again to concern. "Can I help you?" Anna asked. "You're hurt," and she stepped forward to help.

"T-watch out!" Tan yelled from the top of the hole.

Glancing at Tan, Anna asked Pat again, "Can I help you?"

Pat appeared helpless, but he still hesitated. Then finally he replied, "P-you are still my prisoner." He turned towards the other soldier and shook him. No response. As Pat examined him, he realized that the soldier died from the fall. "P-he is dead! P-now, you are going to pay," he growled.

"T-no, we are not," Tan responded from the edge of the hole, looking down at them.

"Be quiet, Tan," Anna said. Then she told Pat, "I am here to help you."

Pat tried to hold in his pain, wincing. He was not yet able to trust Anna.

"T-why don't we pull him out now? T-Anna, T-check to see if he is still secure," Tan suggested as she got ready little feet secure in the dirt.

"Good idea," Anna replied. Then Tan and Anna worked together to get Pat out of the hole.

"P-you are my enemies." Pat said, but his vigor was gone. He lay down on the ground and closed his eyes. He could hardly walk because his legs hurt so much from the fall. He winced in pain.

"We are going to help you," Anna said in a gentle voice.

"T-watch out for him!" Tan warned.

"We cannot run forever. I'm going to help him." She began to grab him by his arms and then she shot a look at Tan. "Are you going to help me?"

Tan rolled her eyes and said, "T-let's make a bed by weaving the rope between two sticks."

Anna found two strong, long sticks and she and Tan began to wrap and weave the rope between the sticks like a crude stretcher. When they were done, Pat rolled over on top of the girls' handy-work. Tan and Anna lifted the front and began dragging the stretcher through the forest to the Puttin warriors.

We've got to help them!

Chapter 8

Back at the camp, the Puttins had brought out their java juice to celebrate the victory. One of the Puttins saw Anna and cried out, "P-there she is! P-let's get her."

As she and Tan came closer, another Puttin said, "P-they are carrying our leader! P-we need to help him."

Anna heard Tear shout, "T-run! T-run! T-what are you doing? T-idiots!"

Anna and Tan ignored him and approached through the trees on the path, dragging Pat behind them. As they came closer to the raiding party, Tan blurted out, "T-we're dead!"

The little pink fly was on Anna's shoulder, squealing in fear for her friend's safety.

The warriors approached; Anna set Pat down and began to raise her hands in surrender, and Tan did, too. Two more warriors advanced with swords in hand. "P-step away from our leader!"

"T-oh no," whispered Tan. Anna could see that Tan believed this was the end.

Just as Anna's heart began to race, Pat said, "P-these ladies saved my life!"

The soldiers were so stunned that you could hear a pin drop. "P-take me over to the other soldiers," Pat continued. He gestured for the soldiers to carry him.

The soldiers did as they were instructed. When they got to the raiding party, Pat said to Anna, "P-I owe you my life. P-as a result you are no longer my prisoner, but my guest."

Anna responded, "Then stop the war between you and the Little People. Please stop the killing!"

"P-I want to grant that, but P-we need the honey that the rainbow flies make," he answered.

"T-you have no rights to it," Towel yelled out.

"P-if the Little People grant us access to the fly cave, we can make peace," Pat stated.

Anna looked to Tear, "Why don't you grant them access and stop the stupid killing of both sides?"

Tear thought about it and then said to Pat. "T-if you stop the killing, T-we will grant you access to the fly cave." Then Tear continued, "T-if we agree on this, you must let my people go. T-agreed?"

Anna was thrilled to see Pat scratch his fat belly and say, "P-agreed!"

Tear and Pat shook hands; the pact was made.

Tear told Towel, "T-in the morning, we will help carry Pat to his village and T-we will accompany him there."

"T-yes, sir," Towel said.

Towel turned to Anna and said, "T-I am sorry for not trusting you." Towel put out his hand, but Anna ignored his hand and hugged him instead.

The little pink fly landed on Towels head and chirped gleefully.

Tan smiled her approval, "T-that's better."

"P-prepare a meal, and build a fire," ordered Pat. "P-let's settle down for the evening. Tomorrow, at Puttinville, we will celebrate our pact."

"T-one of you, go help Pat," Tear ordered the once-captive-warriors.

Anna smiled as she watched Towel volunteer. She saw him approach Pat who was still laying on the stretcher. "T-are you okay?" Towel asked Pat. Towel gave him some water and helped carry Pat to the campfire.

"P-my leg hurts but I am okay for now," Pat replied, wincing in pain.

Anna and Tan helped the Puttins prepare the evening meal. When it was ready, everyone sat down to eat and talk.

Anna asked Tear and Pat, "Did you know each other before there was war between the tribes?"

"T-yes," replied Tear. "T-I remember when we were young and T-how we played together at Puttinville. T-has Puttinville changed?" Tear asked Pat.

"P-not much has changed." Pat, reassured him. "P-and,

you all will be our guest tomorrow. P-we will dance joyously together and laugh."

After the meal, almost everyone went straight to bed and slept soundly, safe in the knowledge of their newly found peace.

Tan and Anna spoke to each other quietly in their tent before sleeping. "T-you have given us a gift that I can never repay. T-the gift of peace," Tan told Anna with tears in her eyes.

Anna grabbed Tan's hand and squeezed it gently.

"T-I apologize for my attitude of not wanting to help Pat."

"I understand, and I'm sorry I told you to be quiet," Anna responded. "You are a good friend." They hugged each other, and then giggled, a little embarrassed.

"T-let's get some sleep," Tan suggested as she brushed her tears off with a smile.

P-Puttinville!

Chapter 9

The next morning, Towel sent Tom and ten Little People warriors back to the Little People's village to announce the peace treaty with the Puttins and to start rebuilding. Tom and his mate Tia would organize a peace treaty celebration for the Little People.

While the Puttins packed up the camp, Pat sent some of his warriors back to get their fallen comrade. They wanted to carry him back to the village in order to give him a proper burial.

Finally it was time to go. Pat gave the order, "P-let's go to the Puttin village where we can celebrate!"

Even though there was some sadness for the fallen Puttin warrior and the destruction at the Little People's village, the main emotions were jubilee and celebration as they walked together toward Puttinville.

Pat and Anna walked next to Tear. "P-you will be my guests. P-you can celebrate the treaty with me!" Pat exclaimed. "P-I'm so glad we have peace at last."

Tear looked over at Anna, "T-thanks to Anna," he commented, sending a smile Anna's way.

Anna smiled back and said, "I hope we are almost there!"

They made good time, and a few hours later they reached Puttinville. Once again, the forest prevented Anna from seeing ahead. She got her first sight of Puttinville as she stepped between two bushes. Anna saw 100 tents in an open clearing, and a big rock at the edge of the town. The craggy, rough rock was about 10 feet tall and 10 feet wide. The Puttins conducted their government meetings and their celebrations at the Rock of Peace.

"P-Puttinville!" called one of the soldiers.

"Hm, it is just like the Little People village," whispered Anna to her faithful pink fly.

The pink fly chuckled a chirping response.

Towel blurted out, "T-we're almost there! T-I remember visiting Puttinville as a child, before the Puttins and Little People were enemies!" he told Anna in excitement.

When the group arrived at the edge of town, startled Puttins ran to meet them.

"P-Peace at last!" Pat yelled. Then he gestured for the Puttins to gather around. "P-this young girl and her P-company helped me. P-they saved my life! P-we made peace with the Little People. P-there will be no more war!" And Pat grabbed Tear's hand and raised it high in a show of friendship.

The Puttins gazed in stunned disbelief. Then, one of the males in the crowd stepped forward. "P-I am Punk and my mate is Patty."

He gestured for the Puttin lady next to him to speak. She smiled joyfully and asked, "P-are they going to let us go to the fly caves?"

"T-yes, we are. T-we are all tired of war, and of hating Puttins. T-we all want peace," answered Tear.

The whole crowd broke out into a spontaneous cheer.

P-peace, P-peace at last!
P-to the Rock!
P-to celebrate!

A Puttin female introduced herself to Tan and Anna, "P-so, P-you are the person to thank for our newly found peace." She stared at Anna.

"Yes, or I think so," Anna responded shyly.

"P-my name is Putree," she said. Putree was a pretty, young female in her twenties. She was round like all Puttins, and she had a cute, short hairdo, big brown eyes, and long lashes.

"T-my name is Tan and this is Anna," Tan responded.

Patty called to Putree, "P-we need to help Pat to his tent."

Putree turned to Anna and Tan, "P-can you give us a hand?"

They all grabbed a corner of Pat's stretcher and headed to Pat's tent. On the way, Patty asked Pat, "P-how do you feel?"

"P-I am in a lot of pain but I am fine," Pat stated firmly trying to appear strong.

"P-we are taking Pat to his tent to treat his wound with special healing water," Putree explained to Anna.

The pink fly flew over to Pat's shoulder and made noises of encouragement.

"You'll be fine," Anna told Pat, her heart tender.

The females came and entered Pat's tent, they laid him on his bed and began to pour healing water on Pat's injury.

"T-look, the injury seems to be getting better," Tan observed.

"P-yes," said Patty.

Putree nodded at Tan and Anna and gestured for them to leave the tent, "P-our leader needs rest for tonight. P-come, let me show you around our village."

"T-that will be fun," Tan responded.

Anna grinned in anticipation of the tour.

P-let's play kick!

Chapter 10

Putree suggested, "P-let's play kick, P-it's a Puttin game."

Anna happily responded, "Yeah, what fun!"

Tan went along with them when they went out to the open clearing. When they reached the middle of the meadow they saw a hole just big enough to fit a ball into it. Putree scooped up the ball sitting next to the hole.

She explained the game, "P-the object of the game is to kick the ball into the hole. P-one person kicks the ball and the other person tries to block the ball."

"T-I will try," Tan volunteered.

Anna sat on the sidelines to watch the game and the fly kept her company.

Putree kicked the ball. Tan saw it coming and tried to block it. But the ball whizzed past her and flew straight into the hole before Tan could block it. Putree's skill came from playing this game all the time.

"P-is that the best you got?" Putree goaded Tan.

Tan, frustrated, kicked the ball as hard as she could.

"Watch out!" yelled Anna, but too late.

The ball hit Putree on her big tummy, "Oof!"

Tan and Putree glared at each other.

"Are you okay," Anna asked.

"P-I am fine," Putree answered. She ignored Tan who stood with an innocent look on her face.

"Let's go for a walk," Anna suggested. She hoped to ease the tension sparking between Tan and Putree.

As they headed for the village Anna commented, "This is just like the Little People's village only they have tents instead of huts. My fly friend and I noticed as we came into town earlier today."

"P-yes, our villages are simple but we Puttins prefer tents over huts. P-they are easier to build and to move," Putree explained.

"T-I'll take my hut over your tent any day; plus huts are cozier," Tan declared.

"What a fun afternoon," commented Anna sarcastically.

Tan and Putree both turned and made a funny face at her.

They soon approached the edge of town. "P-here is the Saloon," Putree said.

As they passed the building Anna got a funny look on her face and said, "Do you smell something funny?"

"P-no, it must be your imagination," Putree said a little too quickly.

They continued walking, and ten minutes later they came to Putree's tent.

"P-welcome to my tent, so very cozy," Putree commented

with a sly grin. "P-the place I call my home," she said with pride.

Tan goaded her a bit, "T-second rate living space, if you ask me. T-when you come to the Little People's village, I will show you my home."

"P-what!" Putree exclaimed.

Anna laughed and pretended to mother them, "There, there. Let's all get along."

Everyone laughed.

The three girls talked, drank water, and ate some vegetables that Putree had prepared that morning and left in her cool-box.

"P-good stuff," Putree raved.

"T-it is okay," Tan teased. "T-I'll show you our plants which are even better quality." Tan responded.

"P-have it your way then," Putree sulked.

Anna laughed to herself as she changed the subject, again. "Let's do something."

"P-maybe we can go help set up at the Rock of Peace," Putree suggested.

"T-I don't know what's so great about that big rock," Tan commented quietly.

"P-what did you say?" Putree asked Tan.

"T-oh, nothing. T-let's go," Tan answered.

When the three ladies arrived at the rock and started to help prepare for the party, a little Puttin girl ran up to Putree and asked, "P-where is momma?"

Putree replied, "P-Poo, she is attending to our leader."

Putree smiled at Poo and introduced her to Anna, her little pink fly, and Tan.

"P-hi," Poo said, and then ran off on her cute chubby legs.

Putree, Tan, and Anna helped set up for the celebration in the afternoon and then rested in Putree's tent until it was time to start. Putree and Tan made an effort to get along.

Puttins enjoy java juice

Chapter 11

That evening the Puttins and their guests gathered at the Rock of Peace on the edge of town. They celebrated peace between the Puttins and the Little People with a huge festival. Towel and Tear built a bonfire in front of the huge rock, and a hundred people danced around shouting:

P-peace, P-peace, P-peace at last!

"What a wondrous time when dreams come true," Anna's eyes smiled in excitement and her little fly friend danced a happy fly dance.

Anna stood with Tear, Pat, Towel, Tan, and Putree next to a table that was a little bit away from the light of the fire. The table held all kinds of food, dessert, and drinks they were nibbling at and enjoying.

"P-how do you like our festival?" Pat asked Towel.

"T-excellent! The elders will tell stories of it around the campfire for ages," responded Towel.

"T-thanks for entertaining us, T-where are Anna and I to lodge?" asked Tan.

"P-Punk and Patty want you to stay with them," Pat replied. He gestured for Punk and Patty to join the group.

Patty walked over to the group with her mate and daughter. She smiled at Anna and Tan and said, "P-my husband and I look forward to having you with us."

"P-so do I," said Poo, jumping up and down with excitement.

Punk smiled, too. Then he picked up his daughter and put her on his shoulders so that Poo could see over the crowd.

Then Pat said, "P-it is time for the ceremony." Pat lit the ceremonial torch on the rock as a signal to the crowd to quiet down and listen. When he held everyone's attention, Pat spoke, "P-we all have Anna to thank for the new union between the Puttins and the Little People."

The crowd cheered in response: P-peace, P-peace, P-peace at last!

Pat gestured for Anna to come forward and make a speech. Anna whispered, "But I don't know what to say!"

"P-it doesn't have to be perfect, P-just be you and relax. P-you will do fine," encouraged Pat.

Anna's fly chirped lovingly as Anna stepped forward and said, "Thank you for this wonderful celebration. You have made me and the Little People feel very welcome. I thank you." Anna curtsied sweetly.

Pat smiled and said, "P-you'll always be welcome here in Puttinville." The crowd shouted their agreement.

Punk put Poo down and she ran and jumped into Patty's arms, "P-I love you mama."

Excitement was everywhere and the party lasted for

hours. When the festival was over, Anna said goodbye to Tear and Pat who planned to stay and discuss the details of the new treaty late into the night. Then she walked with Tan and Patty's little family to their tent on the far side of Puttinville. It was a dark night, so Punk held a torch so they could see as they maneuvered their way between the tents; some tents were big and some were small. Patty carried Poo who was tired. Punk pointed to one of the biggest tents and said, "P-there is Pop's tent and his dad's before him." But, Tan and Anna didn't pay close attention because they were so sleepy.

They finally reached Punk and Patty's place on the edge of town. Their tent was made of animal skins and animal fur, and was quite cozy. Everyone was so exhausted, sleep came quickly to them. Poo slept next to Anna and Tan; they all were quite comfortable.

In the morning Anna, Tan, Patty, Punk, and Poo sat at a breakfast table situated in front of Punk and his mate's tent. They shared a tasty breakfast of meat, vegetables, bread, and java juice. Anna liked the java juice most of all. Java juice caused most of the Puttins to fart when they overindulged.

While Patty, Tan, and Anna were talking, they suddenly all heard a loud, disgusting farting sound.

Patty bellowed, "P-take it to the saloon!" The saloon was located on the outskirts of town and Puttins often hung out there to enjoy java juice and to socialize.

Punk laughed. Poo blurted out "P-that is a good one daddy."

Patty pretended to be annoyed by purposefully ignoring Punk. As she turned her back to her mate, she winked and giggled at Anna.

Towel joined Anna and her group at the breakfast table. "T-how are you?" he asked Anna, his voice and manner gentle. He then smiled at the rest of them.

Pat and Tear also approached the breakfast table. After talking all night, Pat and Tear completed their discussion of the treaty.

"T-Anna, T-we have decided that you need to go to Soul Town where the humans live. T-that is where you belong," Tear stated.

"T-can I go too?" Tan put in. She was growing more attached to Anna as their friendship blossomed.

"T-yes," replied Tear.

"T-I agree, we must go," Towel said.

"P-I will come with you, too," Punk said with an enthusiastic smile.

"P-I want to go along also," Poo complained.

"P-no!" Patty told Poo.

"P-then it is settled," Pat said. "P-Tan, Towel, Tear, Punk and I will accompany you on the journey. P-remember, we will travel through the forest a long way, and we have to stay on the enchanted path (the path that never had to be maintained) to get to Soul Town."

"I'm excited to start our next journey!" Anna exclaimed. She clapped her hands and twirled around, the fly chirping dizzily on her shoulder; but Poo pouted.

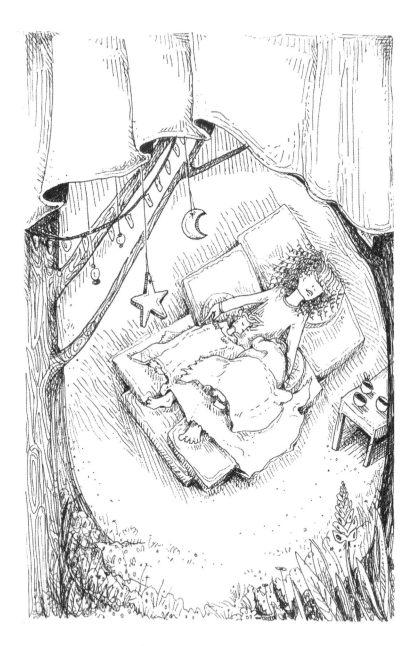

Poo slept next to Anna and Tan

Chapter 12

It took them until mid-afternoon to prepare for the trip. But finally, it was time to start the journey to Soul Town, the home of the humans. The group that formed the expedition walked out to the Rock of Peace to wave farewell to the Puttins.

Anna found tears in her eyes as the group departed to Soul Town. She looked back at the small village and thought about her new friends that she was leaving. But as she stepped into the rainforest in the Land of Dreams, her thoughts turned to her next adventure. They began to follow the path, and the forest slowly engulfed her and her companions.

"T-we are off to see the humans," Tan said in excitement.

Pat added, "P-it'll be a 2-day journey." He led the group, with Towel right on his heels. Punk came next, followed by Anna, and Tan trailed a bit behind. The forest was awesome, and Anna loved looking at the beauty that surrounded her. There is nothing like a tropical rainforest on a sunny afternoon.

Anna took time to look about her as they traveled.

Tan pointed out beautiful plants, trees, and animals. The afternoon passed quickly.

After they were walking for a while, Tan said, "T-let's call the pink fly a name."

Anna stated, "Great idea!" She was watching her little friend's antics.

"T-she is singing," commented Tan as the fly chirped noisily along the path.

"The fly's name will be Pebbles," Anna decided.

"T-that is wonderful," Tan replied.

"Do you like your new name?" Anna asked Pebbles.

"Chirp, tweet, chirp!" said Pebbles.

Pat commented, "P-they are having a good time on this fine afternoon." Tear and Punk grinned.

The evening came quickly, and Towel noticed the growing darkness. He wanted to reach a place to camp. "T-try to keep up," Towel urged the group, attempting to get them to move faster.

"I wish they would slow down," Anna said, the group struggled to keep up.

Pat heard her complaining. "P-it is almost sundown and P-we can stop soon," he encouraged her.

The path curved up and down. Up ahead they saw an open spot in the forest, just big enough to make camp. It was a pretty, little meadow, just off the trail.

"T-that looks good," Tear said.

"P-time to set up camp," Punk exclaimed as Towel and the rest got busy setting up the tents and making the campfire. Pat prepared the meal, and then they all sat down at the fire to eat. Pebbles had a drop of honey to sip. As everyone ate, they discussed Soul Town.

Pat told Anna, "P-Soul Town is nothing like you've seen so far."

"Please tell me more about it," Anna requested.

"T-yes, me too," Tan added.

Pebbles hummed her interest; no rainbow fly had ever visited Soul Town, or been so far away from the rainbow caves.

The fire crackled and popped pleasantly as Pat sat down on a log and took a deep breath. He then began to explain, "P-from the path you'll see a big brick wall with a large gate. P-men will be standing guard. P-as you go in, there is a great arena where jousting and other public events take place. P-the humans are good hosts, and you'll like it there."

"T-I have never seen a human before, besides Anna," Tan said.

"T-I have, from a distance. T-I have seen the great brick wall from the path," said Tear.

Towel chimed in, "T-I saw a human from Soul Town when I joined an expedition through the great forest. T-some of the Little People and humans ventured close to the wolves caves."

"P-it's time for bed," Pat concluded. The group went into their tents and went to sleep.

The next morning, Towel rose up first at 6:00 a.m.,

just as the sun was beginning to rise. "T-get up," he called cheerfully to everyone.

"T-it is going to be a long trip," Tear said.

"P-yes, we need to start. P-the earlier the better," agreed Pat.

After everyone had breakfast and pitched in to clean up the camp, Towel said, "T-time to go," and he began to walk down the trail. The air was fresh and the path was lush. "T-we should reach Soul Town by noon," Towel declared.

The group began to venture down the trail. It was a beautiful hike and everyone was too busy taking in the scenery to talk much. They moved fast, catching the sights and sounds of the forest with its green trees and bushes as they hurried along. Pat led, and Towel was right on his heels in a fast walk.

Then, after a few hours on the enchanted path, Pat pointed out a view of the great brick wall stretching out before them as far as the eye could see. The wall had an impressive brick gate over 15 feet high.

"Wow, look at that wall," Anna exclaimed. Pebbles flew around Tan who stood next to Anna.

"T-wow is right!" Tan agreed.

"T-we need to go ahead and check it out," Towel declared.

Towel and Punk walked ahead, veering off the magical path, to check out the gate to Soul Town. The rest of the group waited beside the magical path. Their resting place was a block and a half away from Soul Town's impressive front gate.

"T-the humans are very gracious," Tear said.

"I hope so," Anna responded as they waited for Towel and Punk to come back.

"T-I'm going to rest over here," Tan said.

"I am, too," Anna agreed.

As Anna and Tan lay on the grass waiting for Towel and Punk to return, Pebbles happily chirped and darted around their heads.

Pat and Tear talked and planned what they must do next. When it was almost evening, the group began to worry about Towel and Punk.

But finally, Punk and Towel returned, and the girls ran to meet them. Punk and Towel started talking at the same time.

"P-let's go, the guards at the gate will take us into the city and find us a place to stay," urged Punk.

"T-O.K., let's go," Towel said eager finally to meet the King of Soul Town.

Pat responded to both Towel and Punk, "P-where is the King of Soul Town?"

"P-this way," Punk said, gesturing to the trail. He led them to the gate.

"P-Soul town was very exciting, I can't wait to see it again," Pat said.

Soul Town

Chapter 13

The travelers approached the outer gate of Soul Town and saw that there were guards stationed there. The city guards were knights, and their silver armor shone brightly. Their swords and shields were laid down right beside them.

Towel walked right up to the guards and said, "T-these are my companions."

"P-where is your king?" Pat asked.

"This way," a guard responded.

The silver knight led them inside the doors. The travelers observed a huge arena, fit for activities and events. Anna was awestruck! There was an open area, and a brick wall that separated the fans from the participants. Guest seating encircled the arena.

As the group moved forward, they observed that the arena was empty except for two men with swords and shields. They were sparring in the open area. "We must wait here," the knight ordered.

"Charles, watch your parry," shouted one of the fighting men as he appeared to get the upper hand, backing up the man called Charles.

"You won't get me, Sire!" Sir Charles taunted as he lunged. But the man blocked the thrust and kept his opponent backing up, and in a gesture that Anna could barely see, sent Sir Charles' sword flying.

The practice fight was over. The opponents bowed in a gesture of respect and shook hands.

The silver knight turned to the travelers and instructed, "Remain here." Then he went over and spoke to the victor.

It wasn't long before the victor approached the travelers. "The guard tells me that you are here from Puttinville," he said.

"P-yes we are," Pat responded.

"You're the leader of the Puttins, aren't you?" asked the man.

"P-yes, I am," Pat replied. "P-and this is Tear, the leader of the Little People."

The man introduced himself, "My name is Edward, and I am the king of Soul Town." Then he asked, "Why are the Little People, Puttins, a human girl, and a pink fly traveling together? And what can I do for you?"

"T-we've figured that since this girl is human, she should be here with her own kind," Tear explained.

The king turned to Anna, "What's your name, and who is your little friend?" he asked gently.

"Anna," she replied shyly. "And this is my friend Pebbles. She is a magical rainbow fly; her honey makes people joyful!"

"Wow, I never saw a rainbow fly before. She is beautiful! Where are you from, Anna?" he asked.

"I was in my bedroom, going to bed, and all of a sudden, I was brought to a magical path where I met Pebbles. The path led me to the Little People, and then to Puttinville, and now here."

"That sounds like quite an adventure," said King Edward. "Come to my castle for rest, food, and drink," the king invited the travelers.

Anna and her companions followed King Edward to the far side of the arena and through another gate; this one opened onto a path leading into Soul Town. The path was a tunnel made of brick, and they soon came to a door. King Edward opened that tunnel door to reveal a lavish entrance. Two guards were stationed there and two more were standing guard in front of a staircase. The group went up the stairs, across a hall, and entered into a dining room.

"Please wait here and be seated," the king requested.

The group sat at a huge table as the king left. Two knights stood quietly guarding each door.

"T-let's get comfortable," said Tan.

"I wonder how long he'll be," Anna wondered. Pebbles rested on her shoulder.

In a little while, the king returned with a woman and a young girl about Anna's age.

"Thanks for waiting, everyone," the king said. "This is my wife Marcy, and my daughter May." The females bowed and joined them at the table. Then they began to talk.

"Who are you," May asked Anna.

Anna replied, "My name is Anna." Then she asked, "What is Soul Town like?"

"Only humans live in Soul Town, and we have a lot to do in our kingdom," May explained.

"Like what?" Anna asked eagerly, and Pebbles chirped in excitement.

"Wow! Is that a rainbow fly?" May asked?

"Yes, this is Pebbles. We met on the magical path near the rainbow flies' home," Anna responded. "She has been a great friend to me."

"She is very lovely," Queen Marcy told Anna. Then she turn to her daughter and said, "Anna asked about entertainment in Soul Town, sweetheart."

"A lot of shopping and events," May replied.

"Also," The King added, "I'm leading a party to the Black Hills."

"What's the Black Hills?" Anna asked.

"The Black Hills is a place where we can see sites that arc awesome; it is a magical place. The magic allows me to see if my kingdom is safe. I go there on a regular basis, and it is time to go again, tomorrow." King Edward explained.

"T-I have heard of this in legend," Tear said.

"You must come with us and enjoy the sights, my friends!" King Edward exclaimed.

Just then, a serving woman entered. She set the table for the evening meal. Other servers brought in fried chicken, mashed potatoes, gravy, broccoli, and apple juice. For desert, they had berries and sugar. "This is my kind of meal," whispered Anna.

Pebbles nibbled on the berries and sugar.

"I thought the Puttins and the Little People were at war, what changed?" King Edward asked the two leaders.

Pat spoke up, "P-Anna saved my life and then made a strong case as to why we should make peace."

"T-she brought our two peoples together," Tear added.

"You are a very special girl," the king told Anna. "Tonight we get some sleep and tomorrow we go to the Black Hills," the king concluded the conversation.

After supper, Marcy showed Tan and Anna to a lovely guest room in the castle, a guard led Towel and Punk to where the guards slept, and King Edward showed Tear and Pat to another guest room in the castle. It had brick walls with a nice fur on the floor, and kingly sized beds to fall fast asleep in.

T-wake up, T-wake up!

Chapter 14

In the morning Towel banged on Anna's door. "T-wake up, T-wake up. T-I brought you some breakfast. T-eat and get ready, and then meet everybody downstairs," he called.

"Thank you, Towel," Anna responded.

"T-yes, t-thank you for thinking about us!" Tan also called out through the door.

As they heard Towel walk away, Anna and Tan looked at each other and grinned. "T-yah! T-let's get the food!" Tan exclaimed.

Anna jumped up to get the food, and Tan prepared the table. Then they both sat down to enjoy the yummy breakfast Towel had provided. They ate fluffy scrambled eggs, a small loaf of bread, creamy butter, sweet strawberry jam, and delicious tea. It was delightful!

"I am so full," said Anna, rubbing her tummy.

"T-me, too!"

Tan got up and started to get ready for the day. "T-let's get ready, Anna."

While the girls prepared themselves for the day, Pebbles nibbled on the left-over strawberry jam and buzzed happily.

"T-I think we're ready," Tan stated calmly.

Anna giggled and taunted, "I'll race you down the stairs!" And she ran out the door.

Pebbles, zoomed past Tan and raced ahead of Anna.

Tan yelled, "T-wait up!" and ran after them.

"I win!" Anna exclaimed when they reach the others.

"T-you turkey!" Tan teased.

The rest of the group laughed at their teasing.

"Good morning, ladies! It's time to go," King Edward greeted them.

Queen Marcy and Princess May stood next to the king. Queen Marcy stepped forward and hugged Anna. "It's been fun getting to know you. I'll see you in a few days." She kissed her husband's cheek, and King Edward blushed.

Next, Princess May stepped forward and hugged Anna. "See you soon, Anna!" Then she turned and waved goodbye to her daddy and the rest of the group.

King Edward waved back, "We'll be back soon." Everyone waved as the queen and princess turned and walked back into the castle.

The king led the group out the castle door that opened into a tunnel. Sir Charles came after the king and led a dozen soldiers; Sir Charles was both the Captain of the guard and the king's friend. After the soldiers came the Puttins and the Little People with Anna and Pebbles, and last came the servants leading pack-animals. Each person carried a pack with supplies, but the pack-animals carried the tents and the water.

The group followed the tunnel which led them straight into Soul Town with its many shops, stores, and brick buildings. As they made their way through Soul Town towards the exit of the township area, the citizens lined the street to waive and cheer at the king and his party. The city guards controlled the crowds.

King Edward waived at his people with pride and joy. Tan and Anna also waived to the crowd as they walked by. They felt excited and a little overwhelmed by the noise.

As the group approached the exit they heard voices from the crowd call out, "Long live the king!" They stepped through the exit and found themselves in a back passageway; after one block they walked through the outer gate. Towel, Punk, Tear, Pat, Anna, and Tan watched as the huge brick gate closed, sealing the back entrance to Soul Town shut.

The group walked a mile on a brick walkway that led from the gate to the magical path. Pebbles entertained them; she danced and chirped as they went along. Finally the bricks ended and the magical path began, the path that never needed any upkeep or care.

As Anna stepped onto the path she declared, "Now, the real expedition begins!"

"T-off to the Black Hills we go," Tan agreed.

"T-let's get moving so we can get there fast!" Towel urged.

"It is two days to the Black Hills," King Edward calmly reminded the group from the front of the line.

The sun shone brightly and it was hot, but they continued down the path with excitement. The expedition enjoyed the beauty of the path as they walked along.

Anna and Tan played with Pebbles; she helped them forget the heat of the sun. Anna couldn't wait to see the Black Hills. "Wow," she thought to herself as she pictured the Black Hills in her mind and remembered King Edward's description of them.

After a while, Anna found herself up front with Pat, King Edward, and Sir Charles who was leading the expedition. She listened to them talk.

"P-are there any dangers in these woods?" Pat asked King Edward.

"Not for many years," the king responded.

"We used to have a problems with wolves," Sir Charles informed Pat, "but we fought them back so they don't venture this far from their dens."

"But just to be safe, we never go to the Black Hills without soldiers as an escort. As you can see, we have 6 soldiers in the rear, and 3 on both sides of our group," King Edward stated.

Anna was glad the soldiers were protecting the group, it made her feel safe.

After a day's walk, the group set up camp in a clearing just off the path. When the sun went down a chilly breeze set in.

The king called out, "Let's get the campfire ready for the night."

Very soon the moon set and the stars came out. The night was crisp, clear, and cold; everyone gathered around the campfire. Excitement sparkled in the air and the Black Hills kept popping up in everyone's conversation.

The group stayed up enjoying themselves until late in the evening. Pretty soon Anna stood up, stretched, and yawned. "I can't wait to see the Black Hills tomorrow," she declared to the group.

King Edward smiled, "I hope that you will enjoy the grand scenery."

"T-I can't wait either!" Tan exclaimed. She smiled at her best friend and winked at Pebbles who rested comfortably on Anna's shoulder.

Towel, next to the fire, smiled and declared, "T-time for bed."

King Edward ordered Sir Charles to arrange the rotation of the night guards.

Anna and Tan slept in the same tent with their little friend Pebbles. They were quite tired and they quickly trailed off to sleep.

The expedition

Chapter 15

The group woke up at daybreak and enjoyed breakfast, which included java juice that Pat provided. Afterwards, everyone except a few soldiers that Sir Charles sent to scout ahead, helped the servants break down the camp.

"T-time to go," Towel called out.

The group ventured down the path; it was a fresh new morning. Tear and Towel went with the scouts, and other soldiers guarded the main group. Tan and Anna sang with Pebbles, and Pat smiled at the three.

"P-what a wonderful day," Pat commented.

The group walked just about all day. Finally they came to the Black Hills; it was beautiful. During the last two hours of the hike they climbed up to the highest point, a magical place. The air was fresh; the day was perfect. As they approached the top, Anna's heart began to race, filled with the anticipation of what she was about to see.

Anna stepped forward for her first look and gasped softly to herself, "We can see the entire Land of Dreams!"

Tan was not silent, she threw her hands up in the air and said, "T-wow!"

Pebbles started darting back and forth between people, chirping in their ear and sharing their excitement. Tan said, "T-there is Pebbles, tweeting around."

As they enjoyed the scenery, Towel commented, "T-there is nothing like this in our village."

"T-I agree," Tear responded.

As Anna and Tan stood on the overlook and played with Pebbles, they had a perfect view. They gazed in awe, and couldn't stop smiling.

"P-how do you like it?" Punk asked Anna.

"Grand!" Anna responded.

Pat spoke with excitement to the king, "P-few Puttins have ever ventured this far!"

"Something for you to tell your people about," King Edward responded.

As the servants started to set up camp, Sir Charles ordered soldiers to stand guard. King Edward moved off by himself to look out over his kingdom. The magic would show him if his kingdom was safe.

Anna watched the king as he let the magic work and gazed out over his land. For many years the king had seen only safety for his people. But today Anna watched as the king's face fell in sadness. "Oh no," said Anna. "What is wrong?"

"The wolves were on the move!" King Edward told her sadly.

King Edward called Sir Charles, Pat, and Tear to himself to discuss how to handle the safety of the group on their return to Soul town. They had high hopes of getting home without seeing a wolf; after all, they hadn't seen one on their way there. Sir Charles left to go speak to the soldiers and set their plans in motion. The king, Tear, and Pat joined the group around the campfire.

King Edward stood and addressed the group, "Today, the magic showed me danger for my kingdom. The wolves are on the move! I need to get back to Soul Town to prepare for an attack. I did not see any immediate danger to us tonight. But we need to get to sleep early so that we are well rested for a difficult march in the morning."

Sir Charles stood and said, "The soldiers are standing watch four at a time."

"Excellent!" the king responded. "Now, everyone, it's time for bed."

The wolves are on the move

Chapter 16

The next morning the group ate breakfast, packed up, and started back down the hill to return to Soul Town. The soldiers guarded the group on the path. Six soldiers in front and six in back of the servants, travelers, and the king. Others in the group were also armed and ready to defend.

Punk walked close to Sir Charles and King Edward to participate in the defense of the expedition. Tear and Towel walked closely to Tan and Anna, and Anna was glad for the extra protection. Pebbles chirped notes of comfort and joy to her friends as she flew behind them.

The company moved fast, and soon reached the bottom of the hill. After a short break, they quickly followed the magical path towards Soul Town, and Anna started to wonder if she could keep up.

"I hope that we get there in one piece," Anna said softly to Tan.

"T-you and me both," Tan responded.

Tear smiled and reassured them, "T-we will protect you."

"T-yes, we will." Towel encouraged the ladies.

Anna smiled back, believing them.

Up towards the front of the travelers, Punk heard a wrestling noise. He alerted King Edward, "P-I sense danger."

Everyone stopped and waited. King Edward and the soldiers scanned the scene. Then they also heard the wrestling in the underbrush. It looked like someone was moving there.

"Go check it out," The king ordered one of his soldiers.

The soldier stepped towards the underbrush to check the situation out. He was carrying a shield with a long sword, and a dagger with a very wicked tip was ready on his belt. The group braced themselves as the soldier approached the underbrush.

All of a sudden, a wolf jumped out at the soldier! Although the soldier quickly swung at the wolf with his sword, the wolf was too quick and clever, and the soldier missed. Then, the wolf darted back into the underbrush and was gone.

"A scout!" Sir Charles yelled, "Where there is a scout, there is a pack!"

Towel started to chase the wolf through the underbrush, but Tear ordered Towel to stay with the group.

King Edward ordered, "The scout will be back with his pack, so we need to go forward on the path to find a good place to defend ourselves against the wolves."

They hurried one mile up the path. "Here is a safe

spot for us to guard against a wolf attack," King Edwards exclaimed.

Pat nodded his head in agreement and said, "P-we need to prepare."

Tear inspected the camping spot. It was a large meadow.

"Let's get to work, the wolves are coming," instructed the king.

So, they put the campsite together and everyone helped to build a crude rock wall that surrounded and protected them. Since the place they chose was open on every side, the wolves couldn't sneak up on them. They had plenty of arrows to defend themselves.

While the preparations were taking place, Anna and Tan were feeling worried and anxious. Pebbles, sensing Anna's fear, cuddled against her in her shirt pocket. The girls stopped working for a moment to look up and gaze at the Black Hills. "T-wow! That's so beautiful," Tan said to Anna.

After everyone finished setting up the camp, Anna approached Tear and Pat and said, "Thanks for all you both have done for me, it's been fun."

"T-we're not dead yet, stay with Towel. T-he's a great warrior," Tear replied. And then, since it was getting dark, he encouraged them to get some sleep.

Anna and Tan walked together to their tent. They were comforted by the knowledge that soldiers stood guard outside the sleeping area, arrows ready, behind a wall made of rocks and mud.

In the tent, Tan told Anna, "T-I'm glad that we are friends. T-you have given the Little People peace. T-and I thank you for that. T-good night."

"Good night," whispered Anna. They both fell asleep.

Soldiers stood guard

Chapter 17

It was early the next morning when they heard wolves howling all around them.

"To arms," one of the soldiers ordered. The human soldiers rushed to their stations, arrows ready, just as 100 wolves rushed forward.

"Ready," King Edward ordered. Arrows were aimed. "Fire!" A wave of arrows hit some of the wolves and they fell, mortally wounded.

"Ready," the king ordered again. "Fire!" More wolves fell dead. Now the pack was startled and fled.

"They'll be back," Sir Charles said grimly.

"And with more help," King Edward added.

"We need help. Let's signal the Great King," Sir Charles advised.

"Yes," King Edward agreed, "we need to signal him, to be on the safe side."

Each of the soldiers took an arrow and lit it. Then, at the king's signal, they shot it into the air.

King Edward prayed to the Great King to speedily intervene.

Great King in the city of the Clouds,
Please come to our aide!
Great King of all,
We need you!

Everyone heard the growling of wolves.

"T-they are coming back," Towel shouted as he readied his arrow.

"Ready," the king shouted. Snarling wolves came rushing towards the group. "Fire!" The wave of arrows laid into the wolves. Some fell, but they were more determined this time. "Again!" and more fell.

A wolf leapt over the hastily built wall! "T-you're dead, you turkey!" Towel yelled, then he stabbed it.

"Fire!" the king shouted again. Another wave of arrows struck the wolves.

"T-there are too many of them!" Tear yelled to Pat.

"P-if I'm going down, I'm going down fighting," Pat yelled back.

Just as the wolves began to overwhelm the group, there was a massive explosion. The Great King and his warriors were coming!

Anna's eyes lit up as an angel with a brilliant sword appeared in the middle of the wolves.

"Glory to the God most high!" the angel shouted, then plunged his sword into the nearest wolf.

"For the Great King!" another angel yelled, as he appeared and struck down other wolves.

Fairies joined the fight. One fairy warrior appeared next to Anna. He winked at her before waving his wand at a wolf. A light flashed and the wolf was thrown back! Then the fairy struck the wolf down with his sword.

There was thunder and lightning, and then a golden chariot appeared that seemed to be floating on its own cloud.

This was too much for wolves! As they fled, the warriors' eyes blazed with victory. They cheered, "We won! Glory to God most high, and to his servant the Great King!"

An old, angelic man with white hair stepped off the chariot. Two fairies flanked the man on both sides. He spoke, "I am the Great King of the City of the Clouds."

King Edward bowed and said, "Thank you for your help, my Lord."

The Great King acknowledged the thanks, nodding his royal head slightly, and smiling kindly. Then he commanded Anna to come forth.

Anna stepped out timidly, "Hello, G-G-Great King."

"Do not be afraid. I am pleased to see all that you have done here in my magic land. You have brought peace to the Little People and the Puttins. You have created friendships that will last a whole lifetime. But, now it is time for you to go back to your world," the Great King told her. "After we celebrate this victory, you must say goodbye."

A huge table appeared

Chapter 18

The Great King used magic to clear the battlefield of all the dead wolves. Then he waved his hand and a huge table appeared with chairs enough for everyone to sit down.

"Extraordinary!" King Edward exclaimed in appreciation. And everyone looked in amazement at the Great King's magic, exclaiming in wonder.

P-now we don't have to clean up those dead wolves!" Punk said in relief. "P-awesome."

"Let's begin to prepare for the celebration by building a bonfire," King Edward suggested.

Everyone liked that idea and started pitching in.

Towel playfully instigated some trouble. He took a twig and poked Punk in the tummy, "T-I can kick your butt, fat man."

Punk replied "P-bring it twerp!"

Towel jumped on Punk and they both hit ground rolling. As they wrestled, everyone took bets.

Pat yelled, "P-get that runt!"

Over the cat-calls and cheers, Tear yelled in Pat's ear, "T-like the good old days!"

Pat just grinned and gave a thumbs up.

Towel started to get the upper hand, then Punk farted. They both stopped wrestling, overwhelmed with the aroma. Everyone in the crowd pinched their noses and laughed.

"Who won?" Anna asked, innocently.

"T-who cares?" Tan replied.

Punk jumped up and exclaimed, "P-Punk took the day!" Laughter broke out all over again.

Everyone finished gathering wood; it was piled up high. Rock, the same fairy warrior who winked at Anna during battle, waved his wand at the wood and brilliant flame ignited.

"Are you ready for a celebration?" the Great King asked everyone with a grin.

"P-yes we are!" Pat responded.

"P-but, we need to prepare the food," Punk worried.

The Great King smiled at Punk, and then waved a hand over the table. There was a flash of light, and everyone saw a feast laid out before them. There was something for everyone, even Pebbles had a tiny bowl of her favorite nectar.

"P-Java Juice!" Punk exclaimed, "P-and it's made just right." Punk smacked his lips.

"And little cakes, just the way my mom makes them!" Anna said in delight.

"My favorite ham," said Sir Charles, "delicious!"

The angels and fairies helped to pass the food around,

and served with joy. Even the servants were served this time and enjoyed their favorite foods at the Great King's magical table.

"T-wow, this is so wonderful," Tan said to Anna. Then Tan added, "T-I am going to miss you, Anna."

"I will miss you too," Anna answered, and tears glimmered in her eyes.

Pebbles looked up from sipping her nectar, and chirped encouragement to both of them.

Everyone ate until their tummies were full.

"Now it is time for a show," the Great King announced.

First they had a Fairy chorus. It was so exciting that Anna couldn't stop Pebbles from singing along. At the end of their last song, Rock waved his wand and fireworks exploded in rainbow colors.

"This is awesome," Anna said close to Tan's ear, over the noise of the fireworks.

Next, an Angel sang a beautiful song. The music touched Anna and her companions deeply; it made everyone think of their loved ones.

A beautiful unicorn trotted forward; Anna was amazed when he began to speak. Friends, my name is Patience, and I will recite a poem for you:

We Celebrate the City of the Clouds and the Land Of Dreams

Life and joy,
Victory and peace,
Honor and loyalty,
We celebrate!

King Edward,
His loyal subjects,
Risk to make Soul Town safe,
We celebrate!

Pat and Tear,
Their renewed friendship,
Newly won peace treaty,
We celebrate!

Our Great King,
His rule over all,
Wisdom and compassion,
We celebrate!

Young Anna,
Her friendship with Tan,
Her courage and her heart,
We celebrate!

"Anna, none of these things we celebrate could have happened without you!" stated Patience, and then he bowed to her in the special way the unicorns do. Anna blushed as she observed all eyes on her. "Thanks for this wonderful program," King Edward said to the Great King.

After the celebration concluded everyone went to bed. Tan and Anna slept in the same tent. "T-I will think of you often, T-you're my friend," Tan said, and she hugged Anna fiercely. Pebbles chirped agreement.

The girls stayed up and talked most of the night. They made an effort to enjoy every minute because they knew that Anna would return to her own world in the morning.

When morning came, Sir Charles tapped on their tent and called, "It's time to wake up; breakfast is ready."

A sleepy Anna replied, "Thanks."

Tan also replied, "T-we'll be there, T-thank you." She yawned and stretched.

After they got dressed, they approached the table and sat down. Anna's closest friends were waiting to eat with her. Tear passed them plates that held eggs, toast, and cherries. And Punk gave each of them a mug of java juice.

When they finished eating, Punk said, "P-we love you Anna."

"P-you will always be welcomed in Puttinville," Pat added in. Both Puttins managed smiles for Anna.

Tear said, "T-you will always be welcomed in the village of the Little People."

Towel came up and gave Anna a big hug and Tan said, "T-I hope I see you again."

King Edward and Charles both said, "Goodbye," and shook her hand gently.

The Great King walked up to the group and said, "It is time to go back your world, Anna."

Pebbles hid in Anna's pocket. "I'll always remember you!" Anna cried out to her friends.

"T-I'll remember you, too," Tear said.

"P-so will I," put in Pat.

"T-and I'll miss you, too," Towel added.

Tan cried as she hugged Anna one last time, too choked up to say goodbye.

"Now it's time," the Great King said. And as Anna stepped forward, the Great King waived a hand, and an all-consuming light engulfed Anna.

The next thing she knew, she woke up in bed, in her room. She was so excited she ran into her parent's room and exclaimed, "Mom, Dad, guess where I've been!" And Pebbles chirped joyously as she ran. The End

"Mom, Dad, guess where I've been!"

The magic shows the King danger.

About the Author

Darryl Deshun Bullock loves Jesus and his family. He enjoys living in Washington State with his wife, two daughters, and pets. God blessed Darryl with an active imagination; he constantly works to create new worlds and wonderful stories. Darryl draws the reader into his stories and introduces characters who become dear to the heart.

Printed in the United States
By Bookmasters